This Book Belongs to

EX LIBRIS

Erik J.

D1307411

Mr. Flip Flop

By the author of

RUFOUS REDTAIL

ANGELO THE NAUGHTY ONE

Mr. Flip Flop

BY HELEN GARRETT

ILLUSTRATED BY GARRY MacKENZIE

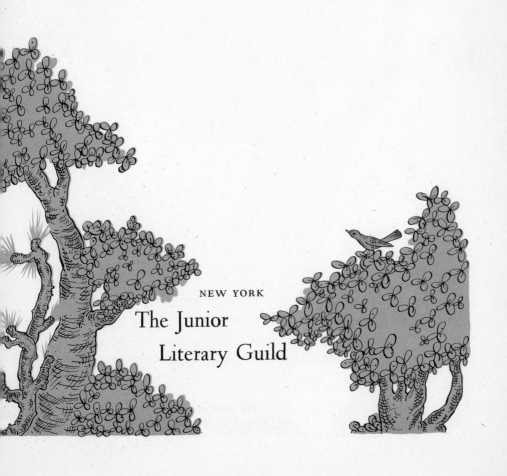

NEW YORK
The Junior
Literary Guild

The story of Mr. Flip Flop
is dedicated to
my friend
Mary Card
who once lived in a beautiful big barn
and
knows and likes all kinds of children

Once upon a time there was a man named Mr. Flip Flop. He lived in a barn halfway between some thick woods and a little village. He lived there so that when the bears came out of the woods he could run into the village. And when the tax collector came out of the village he could run into the woods.

Mr. Flip Flop had been a circus clown who could turn wonderful somersaults in the air, but when his hair turned white as a snowdrift on the day he was sixty-six-and-a-half years old the circus manager told him he was too old to be a clown any more. When Mr. Flip Flop heard this he went to the bank and took out all the pennies he had been saving for years and years, and bought an enormous farm. Right in the middle of the farm was an enormous barn painted a beautiful bright red. He decided to live by himself in this enormous barn so he would have plenty of room to grow old in.

5

Mr. Flip Flop had not been long in the barn before he began to feel hungry. As he had spent all of his money on the farm he had to think of something to do very quickly. He had to think of something to do before supper. So, quicker than snippit, he decided to sell half his farm. He did not need acres and acres besides his barn. That very afternoon he sold the north half of his farm to Mr. Gustavus K. Jounce.

He took all the money from the sale and went to the big red grocery store in the village and said to the manager, "I will give you all this money if from now on you will give me whatever I need to eat as long as I live."

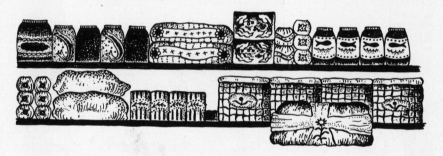

The manager counted the money very slowly and very carefully and said he would do so if Mr. Flip Flop didn't live to be one day over a hundred and ten. Mr. Flip Flop was delighted with this arrangement and hurried home to the barn. When he got there he was the happiest man alive—or so he thought for an hour and a half. He wandered all over the barn, looking at everything and stretching himself as much as he wanted. There was lots of room.

When it grew dark Flippety Flop made a little fire outdoors and sat over it while he cooked some delicious bacon. He ate a red apple and, smacking his lips, said to himself, "I'll never have to work again till I'm a hundred and ten years old. Then I will go back to the circus as the oldest man in the world."

The sun went down and the stars came out and it turned a little chilly. Mr. F. F. stood up and stretched his legs and went inside to bed. But, oh, dear me, where was the bed, and where were the blankets? There were none. They didn't exist. Then Flip Flop looked around for a chair. There wasn't even an old-fashioned rocker or a three-legged stool! There wasn't even a little iron stove to cook on when winter should come with its frosty blasts. Mr. Flip Flop broke into great echoing sobs and threw himself face down on a heap of straw. Finally he went off to sleep with the tears still wet on his cheeks.

In the morning, when he woke up, the sun was shining and the day looked as if it were going to be a lovely one. Mr. Flip felt much better. He dashed out for a plunge in the pool behind the barn. While he was swimming under the clear green water a wonderful idea came to him. So he came to the surface, swam to the shore, pulled on his clothes, quicker than snippit, and ran to the village. There he sold the south half of his farm to Mr. Pickerel T. Bounce, saving for himself only the muddy lane, the big red barn, the pool, and half an acre of thickly matted woods.

As soon as he had the money in hand he dashed to the big white department store on the main street, near the fire-engine house, the police station, and the big post office. He called for the manager of the store and asked him to keep his money. When he wanted things he would come and get them. The manager counted his money very slowly and very, very carefully and said, "Very good. You may buy anything you want as long as it lasts, and if you are not too extravagant you can live to be a hundred and ten before it will give out."

"Whoopee!" Mr. Flip Flop shouted. "That was just what I hoped. I have to go back to work at that age anyway, so a hundred and ten is exactly right."

Mr. Flop threw the manager a kiss over his shoulder and ran down the long flight of stairs into the basement. There he began to order the funniest things imaginable. He ordered yards and yards of rope, feet and feet of wood,

pounds and pounds of nails, and dozens and dozens of iron rings. He forgot all about buying beds and stoves and rocking chairs. He was so full of his wonderful new idea that he could not put his mind on little household articles like blankets and can openers. Gathering his things up in his arms he dashed home at full speed. He flew over the ground so fast that he had to grab the barn door as he went by. He threw his heavy load into a great pile in the center of the barn and gave himself to making his barn the finest gymnasium in the whole wide world. For weeks he worked all day and at night he slept on the clean straw as happy as the rising sun and as warm as toast in the oven.

At last everything was shipshape, and that was the way Mr. Flop wanted it. There were ladders going everywhere, rings hanging by ropes from the high beams, greased poles, jumping boards, and tumbling mats. Mr. Flip Flop looked at his work and wept with joy. It was the most beautiful gymnasium that had ever been seen. He wiped his eyes with the back of his hand and went out and sat on the doorstep to wait for his friends to come.

Now, Flip Flop didn't like people in general—that is, he liked only one kind of people—children. He just loved children! He liked them tall and skinny. He liked them

12

short and tubby. He liked the ones that stuttered. He liked the ones that lisped. He liked the ones with red hair. He liked little girls with freckles and little boys with curls. He liked dirty little children and clean little children— and every kind of little child you ever saw. He didn't have to wait long. They began coming within an hour and they came till all the children of the village were in the barn, jumping, sliding, tumbling, and swinging.

When it got dark, Mr. Flop sent them all home to supper. He took a plunge in the pool and went for a stroll in the woods. He was rather frightened when he thought he saw a bear disappearing in the brush, but he decided that he must have been mistaken and went home and slept on his pile of straw, forgetting entirely that he had meant to buy a bed and blankets.

The next day the children came back and Mr. F. F. was the happiest man in the world. Every day the children came and they became the most athletickest children there ever were. The greatest athlete of them all was a freckled-faced, lean-legged boy whose hair was always getting in his eyes and who had lost one front tooth playing baseball. His name was Ros, which was short for Roscoe, and Mr. Floppety was so proud of him that he wished he were his own son.

Now, Mr. Flip Flop had forgotten one thing. TAXES! If you own land you have to pay taxes. Even if all you own is a big red barn, a pool, a muddy lane, and half an acre of thickly matted woods. Mr. F. F. had forgotten all about taxes! At the end of a year of pure joy he found that he owed taxes, and every year from now on till he was a hundred and ten there would be taxes to pay. Forty-three years of TAXES. Oh, dear me, what could he do?—because there wasn't any money left. Poor Mr. F. F. thought and thought and thought. He thought so hard that he saw stars jumping around in his head.

The first good idea he got was that he might sell the roof off the barn and collect enough to settle affairs with the tax collector for good and all. He had just about decided that this was the very best thing to do when he heard a little girl say that she just loved to come to the barn on rainy days because the roof kept it so warm and dry. Naturally F. F. couldn't sell the roof after that. A few days later he thought of selling the pool behind the barn, but there came a sizzling hot day and one of the boys said he would rather swim in the pool when it was hot than eat a whole apple pie and a quart of ice cream. So he couldn't sell the pool. Finally he thought of selling the woods beyond the pool, but one very little boy said

16

that there were more birds in Mr. Flip Flop's woods than anywhere else he knew. So he couldn't sell the woods. *If* he should sell the muddy lane, he could never go to the village to buy his food and the children could never come and play. What could he do? Dear! Dear! Dear!

Day after day passed, and Flip Flop grew desperate. He squinched his eyes together as tight as he could, he pressed his fists against his temples, he scratched his head and he pulled his ear, but still he didn't know where the money was coming from. But at last, one night when the moon was overhead and a hoot owl was hooting in the woods beyond the pool, there was a loud BANG in Mr. Flop's mind and an idea burst in. Of course. Of course. What a good idea! He would run into the woods and hide whenever the tax collector came and so naturally he would never have to pay any taxes. And that is the way he worked it out. It was such a good idea that he cut a peek hole in the side of the barn toward the village and a door in the side toward the woods.

There was one thing against hiding in the woods, and that was the bears. The woods were full of bears. Several times Mr. F. F. had seen them. Once a whole crowd of them had approached the barn together. Flippy had seen them coming and was so frightened that he ran to the village full tilt. In fact, he ran so fast that he ran out on the other side of the village for a quarter of a mile before he could dig in his heels and come to a stop. It was several hours before he dared to go home.

18

Once he heard them sniff-snuffling around the doorway. He even saw one poke its furry nose into the barn. Flip Flop buried himself under some straw and didn't dare draw his breath. He heard one of them say, "Why, this is a *lovely* barn."

Another voice said, "Let's go in and try the rings."

But a whole chorus of voices exclaimed, "No, certainly not. That would be a very bad thing to do unless Mr. Flip Flop invites us to do so himself." And then they went away.

Mr. F. F. didn't know what to think of this conversation because he thought the bears would eat him if they got a chance. But he did not see them again for a long time, so he began to think they had moved away. Anyway he hoped they had, because he didn't keep a good lookout for them and it would be easy for them to gobble him up when he wasn't looking. Then they would go running back into the woods again, fat and happy over a good dinner of delicious clown.

One lovely Saturday when all the children were in the barn, Ros, the freckled-faced one with the lean legs and one tooth gone, was doing some wonderful stunts. Flippety Flop and the other children were watching him. He swung from beam to beam and turned somersaults in the air. He climbed ladders, slid down poles, and flew across space from one ring to another. He was truly the most remarkablest acrobat the children or Mr. F. F. had ever seen.

Suddenly little Tiddly, the lookout, shouted, "Cheese it, a woman!"

Quicker than snippit, they all dove into box stalls, food bins, threw themselves on the floors of the lofts, or skinned behind posts.

The woman came to the door and looked inside.

"Well, well, if this don't beat all!" she exclaimed, for she was the first grownup to look into the barn since Mr. Flip Flop had lived in it.

Then she cried out loud, "Roscoe! Roscoe!"

A head appeared from a rafter up near the roof. "Yes, Ma?" said Ros, very timid. "Do you want me for something?"

"Yes, I do," Ma said. "I've been chasing all over town looking for you. Your Great-uncle Dane has come to town and he wants to take your picture. But whatever for, I can't imagine."

"Oh, Ma," whined the voice from the rafters, "I don't want my pitcher taken. I'd have to get all dressed up."

"No, you won't," Ma said. "He's the kind of photographer who takes people just the way they are. He says he wants a picture of you to hang in Radio City."

"Whoopee!" shouted Ros. "Then let him come and take me out here." With that he leaped through the air and landed at his mother's feet.

Poor Ma screamed, "Roscoe, what are you doing?"

"Nothin' much," Ros answered, and grabbing some rings he began swinging high over Ma's head till she was dizzy.

"Roscoe, come down," she cried. "Come down this very minute!" But Roscoe just kept on swinging higher and wider.

Then Ma thought she saw faces peeping at her from every direction. With a cry of "For lan' sakes!" Ma disappeared up the lane quicker than snippit.

"Whoopee!" shouted everyone, including Mr. Flop, and the air was full of flying figures. A little girl with curls walked on her hands across a beam. A little fat boy slid down the greased pole upside down. Two tiny boys held hands and swung from ring to ring all the way around the barn. A big girl with braids turned handsprings across the floor. A tall boy hung by his knees from a pole and swung a little girl by her wrists higher and higher like

23

the pendulum of a clock. In the corner a boy was training his dog to climb a ladder and in the center Mr. F. F. was teaching four children to turn flip flops.

The lookout was walking about on his hands and he walked slowly out the door to take a look to windward. "Look out," he screamed, dropping to his feet. "Three at once!" and he dove into the barn. Like magic the children disappeared again.

Flippy squinted through the peek hole, and, horrors, what did he see? The tax collector coming! With a loud wail he burst through the door at the back of the barn and vanished into the woods.

Presently three grown people stood in the doorway looking into a silent empty-seeming barn.

"Well," said a man's voice, "where is Roscoe?"

"Roscoe," called Ma.

"Roscoe," cried the other man's voice, "come out of your hiding."

"Yes, Pa?" returned a little voice up in the air.

All three looked up, yet nothing could they see.

"Come down immediately," Pa said. "Your Great-uncle Dane wants to take your picture."

"You bet," Ros called, and down he flew like a bird from a tree.

"Whoa, look out for yourself!" cried Great-uncle Dane.

"Goodness sakes' alive!" Ma cried. "How can you do such things?"

"Oh, we can all do such things," shouted a lot of little voices, and from every beam, plank, and post appeared a flying or tumbling creature.

"What in the world is this?" Pa cried in astonishment.

"Mr. Flip Flop's Flying Acrobats," everyone shouted.

"Where is Mr. Flip Flop?" Pa asked.

A little rosy fat girl who was swinging over their heads lisped, "I heard him thay ath he dathed into the woodth, 'Oh, dear me, here cometh the tacth collector!' "

Then Roscoe's pa laughed and said, "He doesn't need to be afraid of me. He only owes fifty cents. Let's go and get him."

So everyone shouted, "Whoopee!" and ran into the woods.

"Mr. Flip Flop. Mr. Flip Flop," they all shouted. "Where are you, Mr. Flip Flop?"

But no answer came to cheer them. They looked and looked and looked. Just silence and trees seemed to be in the woods.

Finally the little girl who lisped pushed through some

dense pines, calling, "Mithter Flip Flop. Pleathe, Mithter Flip Flop," and saw before her a ring of ten big brown bears. In the center of the ring sat Mithter Flip Flop looking a little frightened and very surprised.

The bears were saying, "We can't understand why you run away every time we come to see you. We are so eager to be friends and to play in your wonderful barn."

Mr. Flip Flop murmured, just loud enough for everyone to hear, "I thought you wanted to eat me."

"Eat you?" the bears cried in astonishment. "Eat you? Why, we like raspberries and honey, bacon and candy, and even soda pop. But not people!" Then they began to laugh, and they laughed harder and harder until they were all rolling on their backs on the ground.

"I'm very sorry," Mr. Flip Flop said, and he got very

red in the face. "But bears in the circus were very danger-ous. They were known to hurt people."

"Of course, of course," said one old bear at last, sitting up on his haunches, "but that was because they were in the circus. Bears in a circus or a zoo sometimes get ugly, but we are quite different."

29

Another bear pulled himself together and stopped laughing, too. "You'd better come with us," he said, "until that horrid tax collector you've told us about goes away. We can show you a place to hide that is impossible to find. Then we can go back to the barn later—if you will invite us—and have some fun on the rings."

The little girl who was watching them from the pine trees called once more in a trembly voice, "Mithter Flip Flop, come home. Everybody wanth you to come home. A man wanth to take your picture."

The bears all swung around and faced the little girl. "Pictures?" they cried. "We love having our pictures taken. Yessiree! We'll come to have our pictures taken."

"But what about the tax collector?" wailed Mr. F. F. "I owe him money and I haven't any. I shan't have any till I'm a hundred and ten. No, no, I can't go home till he is gone."

"There ithn't any tacth collector," the little girl cried, because she didn't know that Ros's father was the tax collector. "There ith jutht Roth'th father and mother and the man to take the pictureth. Pleathe come back."

"Yes," cried all the bears. "Do let's go and have our pictures taken."

"I'm still afraid," Mr. Flop said mournfully. "One of

those men looked just like the tax collector to me." But he
noticed tears of disappointment standing in the eyes of

the bears, and their fur was tinged with blue. "Well,
well," he tried to say cheerfully, "if you all want your
pictures taken, we'll go back to the barn, but I'm going
to walk behind you and you mustn't let that horrid man
come near me."

Very stealthily, led by the little girl, they started back
through the thickly matted woods. First the little girl who
lisped, then the ten bears treading softly, finally Mr.
F. F., who was trembling in his boots.

But nobody did they meet. The woods were quiet.
Not a rustle could be heard. There was no flutter of girls'
dresses, nor glimpse of boys' tawny hair. At last they
came out onto the cleared land where the pond was and
started up the muddy lane to the barn. They began to be
very cheerful. Flippety didn't tremble any more. The
bears lost their caution and walked jauntily. After a whole

year of trying in vain to introduce themselves to Mr. Flip Flop they had caught him and made friends with him. Now they would have a chance at those lovely trapezes!

They reached the barn door and looked in. Everybody inside was standing, as if made of stone, to have his picture taken. Even the tax collector was trying to look clever. He was frozen in a stiff position like a statue.

"Can't you put some life into it—some expression?" cried Great-uncle Dane angrily. "Radio City doesn't like pictures like that." And then before his eyes, quicker than snippit, there was the greatest movement he had ever seen. The tax collector ran up a ladder and crouched against the ceiling, the children scampered up ropes, and Ros's mother gave a sad little scream and sank in a heap, unconscious, on the ground.

Great-uncle Dane looked into his camera and exclaimed, "Good. Good. That's more like it." But then he turned his head toward the door. His eyes popped out of his head and his hair stood on end, for there, crowded in the doorway, were ten bears and a little girl. He didn't move, so the bears came right in. They came toward him with a hungry eagerness. His legs shook and his heart jumped into his throat but he was rooted to the ground by fear.

"We want our pictures taken," they cried. "We just love having our pictures taken. We'll do the most wonderful stunts for you. Because Mr. Flip Flop says we can play on the rings." They turned around to get his approval, but he was gone.

Mr. Flip Flop had seen the tax collector on the ladder.

He was way back in the woods again, hiding in the top of a high tree, from which he could keep an eye on the door of the barn.

36

"Now, that's a pity," exclaimed the biggest bear. "Mr. Flip Flop is afraid to come home while the tax collector is here. Hasn't anybody got some money to give the tax collector so that Flip Flop can live in peace for a year?"

"Why, sure," cried Great-uncle Dane, coming to life. "I've a little money I could give him. Here, little one, run and give this to your friend." And he gave a handful of change to the little girl who lisped. "Tell him to come back and take charge of these bears before they hurt somebody."

"What?" the bears cried. "Hurt somebody? That's very rude of you. We just came for fun. Whoopee!" With that they grabbed the rings and jumped and swung all over the barn. They slid down slides, turned double somersaults, rolled over and over, climbed poles, and had a marvelous time.

Great-uncle Dane grabbed his camera and took some photographs. Meanwhile the children were peeking out from behind beams and boards, fearful of the wild bears and their antics. But at last one little boy could stand it no longer. He screamed, "Whoopee! Here I come!" at the top of his lungs, grabbed a rope, and swung from one end of the barn to the other. It was Roscoe, of course, the very finest acrobat of them all. Even finer than the bears.

In the midst of Roscoe's flying, Mr. F. F. came in and saw Roscoe's mother still in a little heap on the floor. He picked her up and put her on a comfortable pile of clean straw in the corner. She opened her eyes, still looking a little frightened, and watched the stunts that her boy and the bears were doing. And Roscoe's father watched from where he was crouching at the top of the high ladder. He began to be very pleased, then he felt very proud. Finally he was overwhelmingly delighted with what Roscoe was doing.

"By Jove!" he cried out. "This is marvelous! Mr. Flip Flop, the old rascal, is a wonder. Why, he's made an acrobat out of my son. I'll pay his taxes from now on myself. I'll pay till the day he's a hundred and ten."

Now Mr. F. F. was standing directly under the ladder and heard what the tax collector said. He was so happy that he kissed the tax collector's wife. Then he rushed out and kissed Roscoe and all the ten bears. When the children, who were still hiding, saw him kiss the bears they lost their last shreds of fright and came swinging through the air like Roscoe. What bedlam there was— bears and children flying through space, and Mr. Flip Flop in the midst turning double and triple flips!

Finally Mr. Flippety Flip Flop asked them all if they would like some hot dogs and ginger ale. So the bears and the children, and the grownups, too, built a huge bonfire by the edge of the pool and had a picnic. When the sun set they all went home feeling the happiest they had ever felt in their lives.

Mr. Flop took a plunge in the pool and then sat down in his doorway and smoked a pipe. He looked toward the deeply matted woods and knew that the big brown bears were his friends. That was a new and wonderful thing to know. Then he looked toward the village and knew for the first time that the tax collector was a good man. F. F. smiled into the night, knocked out the coals of his pipe against the door, and went in to sleep on a lovely comfortable pile of straw.